JoJo & Gran Gran

This JoJo & Gran Gran storybook belongs to:

_____

First published in Great Britain in 2022 by Pat-a-Cake
Pat-a-Cake is a registered trademark of Hodder & Stoughton Limited
This book copyright © BBC 2022
JoJo & Gran Gran and the CBeebies logo are trademarks of the British Broadcasting Corporation and are used under licence
Based on original characters by Laura Henry-Allain MBE
Additional images © Shutterstock
ISBN 978 1 52638 3723
1 3 5 7 9 10 8 6 4 2
Pat-a-Cake, an imprint of Hachette Children's Group,
Part of Hodder & Stoughton Limited
Carmelite House, 50 Victoria Embankment, London EC4Y 0DZ
An Hachette UK Company
EU address: 8 Castlecourt, Castleknock, Dublin 15, Ireland
www.hachette.co.uk - www.hachettechildrens.co.uk
Printed and bound in China
A CIP catalogue record for this book is available from the British Library

JoJo & GranGran

FIND A DINOSAUR

pat
a
cake

Picture Glossary

Here are some words from JoJo and Gran Gran's trip to the museum.

JoJo

Gran Gran

Ezra

Hugo

Brontosaurus

Triceratops

shell

museum

woolly mammoth

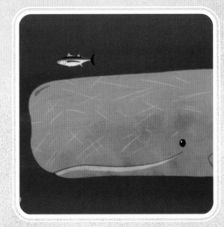

whale

It was a summer day. The sun was shining and JoJo was in the garden with her new binoculars, looking for dinosaurs.

"There!" she shouted.

"It's the Brontosaurus.

Munch, munch, munch!"

Then, she looked amongst the sunflowers.

"Look! A Triceratops.

Stomp, stomp, stomp!"

There was just one more
dinosaur for JoJo to find . . .

She looked around, and then . . .

"Ah ha! Here's Hugo, the Tyrannosaurus rex.

ROAR!"

Then, Gran Gran came outside. "You still haven't found the biggest dinosaur of all, JoJo," she said.

"The GRAN GRAN-OSAURUS! ROOOOAR!"

JoJo squealed and ran away, and Gran Gran stomped after her.

"Playing dinosaurs is fun, Gran Gran," said JoJo. "I wish we could find a REAL dinosaur."

"Well, there aren't any in my garden - I hope!" said Gran Gran. "But . . . I've an idea for a Gran Gran plan!"

"I know a place where we can find a real dinosaur," Gran Gran told JoJo.
"The museum!"

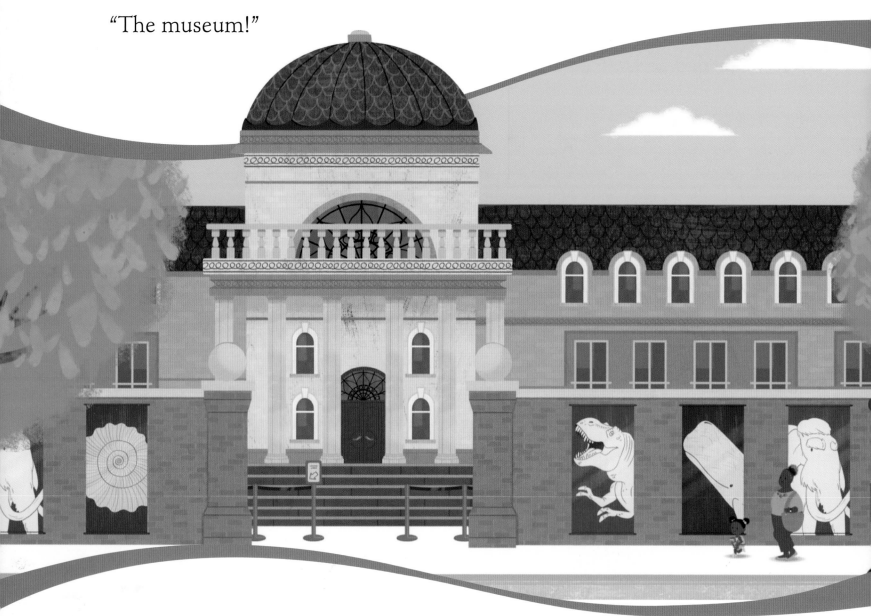

JoJo and Gran Gran headed off to the museum. Outside,
there was a big poster of a Tyrannosaurus rex - just like Hugo!

Inside, JoJo and Gran Gran looked around, but there
was no sign of any dinosaurs. "Gran Gran,
where's the dinosaur?" asked JoJo.

"Hmmm, it's a while
since I've been here,"
said Gran Gran.
She looked around the
lobby of the museum.

"Oh, look, there's my friend, Ezra! He might know where we can find the dinosaur."

JoJo and Gran Gran went over to Ezra to say hello.

"Hello, JoJo!" said Ezra. "Is that your dinosaur?"

"He's called Hugo and he's a Tyrannosaurus rex," said JoJo. "He goes

ROAR!"

Ezra said, "We've got one of those here. Our Tyrannosaurus rex is a bit bigger than Hugo!"

"Is it bigger than me?" asked JoJo.

"Oh yes," said Ezra. "Much bigger!"

"Is it bigger than Gran Gran?" asked JoJo.

"MUCH bigger," said Ezra.

"Is it bigger than the whole museum?" asked JoJo.

"Not quite!" said Ezra, laughing.

Ezra had to dash off to give a tour, so JoJo and Gran Gran didn't have time to ask him where the dinosaur was. They decided to look for it themselves.

"Let's go this way!" said JoJo.

They didn't notice the big, green dinosaur footprints going in the other direction.

JoJo and Gran Gran set off around the museum.

They found a big shell . . .

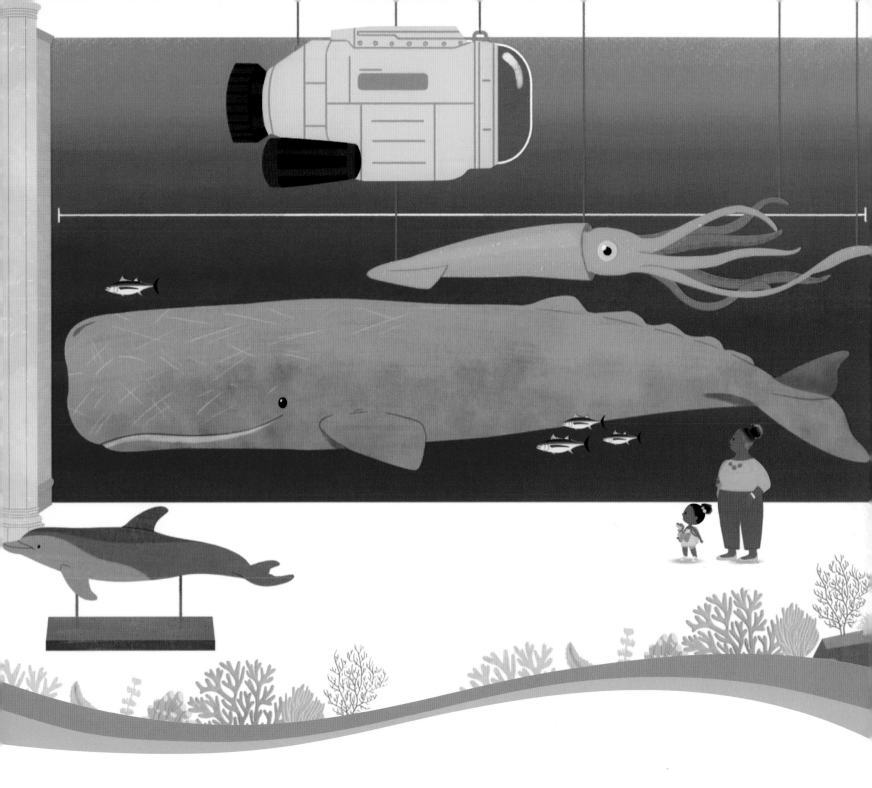

. . . and a REALLY big whale.

They even found a huge
woolly mammoth!

"Are we nearly at the dinosaur?" asked JoJo.

JoJo and Gran Gran carried on looking for the dinosaur.
But when they went around the corner they found that they
were back where they had started!
And there was Ezra again, too.

"Did you find the dinosaur, JoJo and Gran Gran?" asked Ezra.
"No," said Gran Gran, "we got a bit distracted. There are so many
interesting things to see."

"Did you try following the big, green dinosaur footprints?" asked Ezra.
"If you do that, you can't get lost!"

"Thanks, Ezra!" said JoJo. "Come on, Hugo."

So JoJo and Gran Gran set off again, following the dinosaur footprints until . . .

"Wow!" said JoJo.

She pushed a button and the T-rex went ROAR!

JoJo made Hugo roar back at the gigantic dinosaur skeleton.

"This is the biggest dinosaur I've ever seen!" said Gran Gran.

JoJo looked up at the dinosaur skeleton, then down at Hugo.

"But Gran Gran, I thought we were going to

see a REAL dinosaur?" she said.

"This is a real dinosaur," said Gran Gran.

"But it doesn't LOOK like a real dinosaur," said JoJo.

"They're real dinosaur bones," said Gran Gran.

Just then, Ezra came over to chat. "There is a special word for dinosaur bones," he said. "They're called fossils." He explained that dinosaur fossils are all that's left of the huge dinosaurs that roamed the Earth a long, long time ago.

"Amazing!" said JoJo. "Are the dinosaur bones older than me?"

"Oh yes, much older," said Ezra.

"Are they older than Gran Gran?" said JoJo.

"MUCH older," replied Ezra.

"Are they older than everybody in the museum?" asked JoJo.

"Yes," said Ezra, "the fossils are millions and millions of years old!"

"Woah!" said JoJo. "That's REALLY old!"

Gran Gran got out her tablet and everyone did a big ROAR! for the camera.

When they got home from the museum, JoJo got out her toy dinosaurs to play with again.

"Welcome to the JoJo and Gran Gran Museum!" said Gran Gran.

JoJo made the Brontosaurus go

munch, munch, munch.

Gran Gran made the Triceratops go

stomp, stomp, stomp.

"And the best thing in the museum is my favourite dinosaur of all, Hugo the Tyrannosaurus rex!" said JoJo.

"ROARRRR!" went JoJo and Gran Gran.

"Thank you for taking me to the museum!" said JoJo.

"I love you, Gran Gran."

"I love you too, JoJo," said Gran Gran.

Dinosaur Maze

JoJo has left Hugo in the museum. Can you help JoJo find him by working your way through the maze? What else can you see?